~~Scrooge:~~
~~A Life Worth Scribing~~

~~Scrooge McDuck: Pluck, Not Luck~~

~~The Autobiography of~~
~~Scrooge McDuck,~~
~~Volume 2: The Second Hundred Years~~

Yes, that's the one! ↗

Solving MYSTERIES
and Rewriting HISTORY!

By Scrooge McDuck

Fact-checked by
Huey, Dewey, Louie,
and Webby!

For the television series developed by
Matt Youngberg and Francisco Angones

With historical rewrites by Rob Renzetti & Rachel Vine
and mystery-solving illustrations by Niki Foley

DISNEP PRESS
Los Angeles • New York

HUEY, DEWEY, LOUIE

Editorial by Eric Geron
Design by Lindsay Broderick
Darkwing Duck Poster Art by David Cole, Jeremiah Alcorn, and Tanner Johnson
A special thank-you to Suzanna Olson

For information address Disney Press, 1200 Grand Central Avenue, Glendale, California 91201.

Printed in the United States of America
First Hardcover Edition, July 2018
1 3 5 7 9 10 8 6 4 2

FAC-038091-18145
ISBN 978-1-368-00841-9

Library of Congress Control Number: 2018935347

For more Disney Press fun,
visit www.disneybooks.com
Visit DisneyChannel.com

SUSTAINABLE FORESTRY INITIATIVE
Certified Sourcing
www.sfiprogram.org
SFI-00993
This Label Applies to Text Stock Only

CONTENTS

I suppose I should start things off with some sort of introduction to explain why in blazes I'm writing this autobiography. I'll keep it short and get to the good stuff quickly.

Good Reader,

If this warm leather-bound tome caught your eye, it must be because you want to know more about the man, the myth, the legend: Scrooge McDuck. What's my secret to success? Well, prepare to be disappointed, because there is no secret! It was all hard work! Grit! And pluck, not luck!

It was my wit that bested the Greek gods. *Uh, with my help.*

It was my bravery that conquered the mummies. *That time I helped you.*

It was my skill that allowed me to play the greatest golf of my life in a dangerous faerie realm. *Sure, but my shot saved us.*

I've scaled the highest of heights and plunged to the lowest of known depths. *Literally or emotionally? 'Cause today's been a roller coaster for me.*

Every treasure has a story, and every story has a hero. And sometimes that hero was, in fact, me.

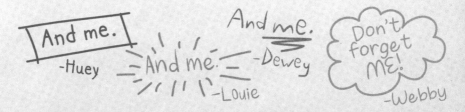

And me.
-Huey

And me.
-Louie

And me.
-Dewey

Don't forget ME!
-Webby

Millions the world over are asking: Why am I writing an autobiography? And didn't I hang up my adventuring top hat? It is true that I took a bit of a break from adventuring. There was a time when I thought that chapter in my life was closed. I kicked up my feet. And you know what I found? I was bored! And lazy! And getting soft! Then I looked around and saw the youth, the great "promise," sitting around, too! Doing nothing!

Is he talking about us?

Well, fine for them! Good! If I'm the only one with the gumption to go after the loot the great civilizations who came before left behind, then phooey to the generation of handout-seeking solly-wags! This autobiography serves as a record of the new adventures that have filled my days, an instruction manual of sorts to show the generations to come just how adventuring is done, McDuck-style.

There are some who ask, "Shouldn't you slow down, Mr. McDuck?" "Aren't you getting a little old, Mr. McDuck?" "Haven't you made enough money, Mr. McDuck?" No! First off, you can never make enough money. It is a mathematical impossibility. Second, Scrooge McDuck has a deep mistrust of one simple word:

RETIREMENT.

Why was I, an otherwise remarkably successful duck, such a dismal failure at retirement? Because I wasn't tired! And I hate so-called leisure time!!! And my _golden years_ should be spent looking for _more gold_, not _spending_ it!

I'll help you spend the money!

My whole life, I've treated every moment as a precious resource, never to be squandered, and now I was supposed to squander _every minute_ on pointless diversions? No thank you, sir! Peddle that nonsense elsewhere.

Unfortunately, Dr. Quackenbush insists that I spend at least an hour each week engaged in something leisure-like. (I negotiated him down from an hour per day, thank heavens.) And I must admit that a wee break now and then does help sharpen the old noodle.

A partial list of my findings: A LIST!

<u>Daydreaming</u>—In a world full of useless pursuits, this is the useless-est! Why should I let my mind wander like some untrained Poodle? Don't confuse this ridiculous waste of time with brainstorming. Brainstorming is setting your mind to attack a problem like a well-trained Rottweiler. Not sure why I'm writing all these dog metaphors, but while I'm on the subject . . .

<u>Dog Walking</u>—Train the lazy mutt to walk itself.

<u>Fishing</u>—Does anyone honestly expect me to sit around waiting for a wee creature to "bite"? I'm proud to say I don't have the patience for such boring business.

Camping—Everyone talks about "roughing it" in the "great outdoors." Please. What's so hard about being outside? Just find a big leaf unclaimed by something with claws, tuck yourself in, and consider yourself lucky you have a bed! In fact, sometimes I leave the mansion and sleep in the yard just to stay sharp! You may think that's strange, but trust me: nothing tests the reflexes quite like a three a.m. dousing from the sprinkler system.

I'd pay to see that!

With whose money?

Museums—Go to a big room (not yours) and stare at a bunch of shiny objects (not yours) behind glass? Maps and artifacts should be used to find other maps and artifacts, not locked up on display!

So THAT'S why Scrooge has been breaking into museums!

Skiing—I hate skiing! Ride up to the top of a hill just so you can race back down it. Oh, and you may die on the way down.

Golfing—I love golfing! Golfing is a walk with a purpose! But there's a problem with relying on golf to see you through retirement: the sport is much more fun if a wager is made. And it's cruel to always be taking some old fool's money because you are an interdimensionally ranked pro.

That never stopped you before. . . .

<u>Movies</u>— The "talkies." Yuck! Forget comedies, dramas, romances, thrillers, and horror movies. All junk the lot of them. But documentaries are another matter entirely. It's a big, wide wonderful world, and even a smarty like me can always learn something new about it. Seemingly trivial tidbits in nonfiction films have led me to amazing business opportunities. It's like getting to work while you're relaxing—the <u>perfect</u> leisure activity!

(<u>Note to self</u>: DO <u>NOT</u> let Dr. Quackenbush know about this.)

Well, that "short" introduction sort of got away from me, didn't it?

I'll rearrange and shorten things in the final manuscript. Probably should end the introduction with some sort of declaration, like . . .

The following accounts are a completely accurate, factual retelling of the exploits I've had since I abandoned the silly idea of retirement and embarked on a new era of unexpected adventures. May they awaken the enterprising spirit in <u>YOU</u>.

— SCROOGE MCDUCK

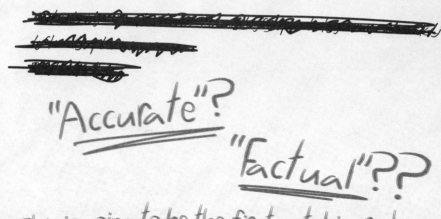

"Accurate"?

"Factual"??

This is going to be the first autobiography filed in the fiction section!

What Dewey means is that there might be a few details you missed in this first draft.

Like the TRUTH!

What we're all trying to say is that we went through and added a little flavor where it was needed.
You're welcome in advance.

New Entry

I should quickly mention the members of my adventuring team, especially the four scrappy young kids, who I must credit with reigniting my thirst for adventure. I am forever in their debt! (If only I could remember their names. . . .)

The One with the Red Baseball Cap—Bit of a know-it-all, this one. Constantly correcting the slightest deviation from the "facts" as he sees them.

"Deviations" from the facts are called lies.

~~Humphrey~~ Hugo? Close enough. At least he stopped calling me Cappy.

(Note to self: Leave room to add a photo after each description.) Don't worry, I've got plenty of ~~secretly~~ ~~taken~~ photos of the whole family.

The brains of the team

Encyclopedic knowledge (and owner of several encyclopedias)

Has earned over 57 percent of all Junior Woodchuck badges in less than three years.

HUEY

↳REALLY?

<u>Bluey</u>—Shows a lot of spunk and a lot more stubbornness. Reminds me of myself at his age—a real pain in the tail feathers.

I'm almost 100 percent positive that his name is Dewey. I think it's short for Ducimer. Or maybe Bartholadew. What? NO!

He might be named after the Dewey decimal system. Who would name their child after an organizational system??!! Well, maybe Huey would. . . . Whatever you say, Bartholadew.

Dewey

Adventurer extraordinaire!!!

Can sword fight and wield nunchakus AT THE SAME TIME!

Trained in battlefield medicine*.

*He can put bandages on the cuts and bruises he gets from playing with swords and nunchakus.

Oooh!
Great superhero name!
Trademarking this!

<u>The Green Hoodie</u>—This one's a slippery character with a quick tongue. Unfortunately, the rest of him moves mighty slowly whenever there's work to be done. He likes money. I admire that.

Lewis? Or maybe it's spelled "Louis"?

No comment. Move along.

Future $ billionaire

Louie

Smooth operator

Mad genius

(<u>COOL</u> mad, not angry mad)

-Double yay!! He knows my name!!!

Webbigail—Not sure where she came from.

BOO!!.. He doesn't know I've been living with him for almost my entire life???

Very enthusiastic. Unfortunately, she's just as enthusiastic about street-corner hot dogs as she is about discovering treasure.

In my defense, treasure is a lot more common in McDuck Manor than street-corner hot dogs.

Ready to take on the world!!

(Can we go explore now?)

Expert in all things Scrooge-related!

Webby!!!

Actually trained in battlefield medicine (by my grandma)

SOME OTHER NOTABLE MEMBERS OF THE TEAM:

Launchpad—My pilot and driver. No sense of personal space, no sense of hygiene. No sense, period. I value sense almost as much as I value cents. So why do I put my life in his hands?

I lost a bundle investing in the "unsinkable" _Titanic_, and then another bundle on the "unstoppable" _Hindenburg_. The minute someone tells you something is 100 percent safe, take your money and your body and run in the opposite direction.

There's no way to guarantee absolute success. That's why I have Launchpad take me wherever I need to go.

No way to fall into a false sense of safety with Launchpad at the controls. It's not really a matter of _if_ you'll crash, but _when_, and how loudly. I like it. Keeps me on my toes.

Should we show this to Launchpad?

He'd probably take it as a compliment.

He takes <u>everything</u> as a compliment.

← This is from his favorite show!

<u>Donald</u>—short-tempered, clumsy, and a spoilsport to boot. Hard to believe that he's the same duck who helped me discover the Seven Cities of Gold.

Whoa. That sounds epic.   And lucrative.

I suppose I know the reason he's changed so drastically. . . . Well, I've spent long enough trying to make things right!

Wait.
What is he alluding to here??

Was Uncle Donald seriously Scrooge's exploring partner???

I keep telling you guys, but you <u>never</u> believe me.

It's time to stop dwelling on all that ancient history. Let's dwell on recent history instead!

Time to (finally) write about my <u>new</u> adventures!

CHAPTER ONE:
That Time I Found Atlantis

After entirely giving up on the idea of retirement from adventuring, I thought it might be best to restart my globe-trotting adventures by warming up with something simple . . . the discovery of the legendary lost city of Atlantis!

(It's not really lost—just really, really hard to reach. But "the legendary really-hard-to-reach city of Atlantis" just doesn't have the same ring to it.)

After some inconsequential detours not worth mentioning,☆ we arrived at the lost city. All that was left was to find the lost jewel of the lost city!

Again, not really "lost" so much as a bit of a hassle to grab. Mostly because, due to some really poor planning by the Atlantians, the whole city of Atlantis is UPSIDE DOWN!

☆Where we fought a kraken, some mermen, and Nimbus, the lord of storms himself!!! ✱

✱You all can thank Dewey for that extra dose of adventure!*

*Thanks for screwing up Scrooge's map and almost getting us killed—not once, but THREE times!!

While it's a bit disorienting to walk through an entire city upside down, it does have its "up" side. The Atlantians designed several elaborate death traps to keep their treasure safe, but since I was walking on the ceilings rather than the booby-trapped floors, I skated right past them.

This is a very lame joke, even for you.

This is not at all how it happened!

The chamber with the lost jewel was another matter entirely. I had to save several of my kin from the clutches of my sworn enemy, Flintheart Glomgold, and, in doing so, was trapped inside while he got away with the jewel. The room began to fill up with water and I would've drowned. But thanks to some quick thinking,* I was able to escape the chamber and secure the <u>real</u> Jewel of Atlantis—a marvelous gem that is also a clean source of enormous electrical power.

This nifty bauble now supplies power for all of Duckburg and has quadrupled the profits of McDuck Water and Electric. Not too shabby an outcome for a little weekend voyage.

* Quick thinking by <u>ME</u>!

Quick thinking by DEWEY!!!

I gotta jump in here, 'cause so many amazing details have been left out.

First, you skipped over all our sea battles on the way to Atlantis—which were amazing. Mermen are so slimy! Your punching fists just slide right off them. And I wish the kraken was better-tempered. He'd be a fantastic addition to the Duckburg Aquarium.

Then you skipped over everything us kids did when we got there. What about our battle with Flintheart's henchmen?? And henchwoman? (Hench-people?)

And the laser beam maze?

And the snakes flying everywhere??

And the whole "prologue" back in Duckburg with Captain Peghook and the Deus Excalibur and—

~~And you lying to your grandma about the whole thing.~~

Weeee don't really need to write that part down. . . .

I'm all for adding our notes to set the record straight, but should we really be taping extra pages into Uncle Scrooge's notebook?

What's the problem? We tape stuff into your books all the time.

You WHAAAAAT????!!!!!??

I suppose it's a little melodramatic to write "I would've drowned." And it's more accurate to write "I _probably_ would've drowned." I might have made it back to the submersible. I've been able to hold my breath for a very long time ever since I spent that summer among the mermen of Bermuda.

Perhaps I should put a section in the book with my tips on holding your breath. . . .

This is crazy dangerous. DO NOT try this at home. Dewey tried and now he can't spell his name.

~~Dewy~~ ~~Deewy~~ ~~Dewee~~ ~~Dewy~~ Of course I can!
Dewey

Practice in a bathtub full of diamonds—This will give you the feeling of being underwater without actually being underwater. Only use your least-precious precious gems. If you use

anything above five carats, the facets get a bit pointy. For an extra sense of danger, pretend your rubber ducky is a man-eating shark.

<u>Practice in a tunnel</u>—Supposedly, if you make a wish and hold your breath while driving through a tunnel, your dreams will come true. It's a bunch of malarkey—HARD WORK makes your dreams come true!—but if it helps you practice holding your breath, then go ahead and believe it.

<u>Practice in your money bin</u>—You can dive under all the coins and . . . Never mind. This really doesn't apply to anyone but me.

<u>Look for air pockets</u>—If you do find yourself actually trapped underwater, you can probably find pockets of air in the hull of the sunken ship you're exploring. If you aren't exploring a sunken ship for gold, I'm not sure why you're underwater in the first place. Don't try this one!

If you make it home safely after escaping underwater cities and battling sea creatures, you've got one further challenge to overcome. . . .

Drying Out Your Waterlogged Money

If you're like me and prefer to pay for everything in cash <u>and</u> you always forget to wrap up your wallet before diving to the bottom of the ocean, then you're going to have a soggy pile of dough to deal with. A few tips:

<u>DO</u> use a clothesline and clothespins. Does a great job of drying bills out and gives them that spring-fresh scent.

<u>DON'T</u> put them in the dryer. Nothing worse than greenbacks with static cling. And don't tell me to use those confounded dryer balls, because they don't help!

<u>DON'T</u> put them in the microwave. There's just no setting that dries them properly. Also, your microwave will definitely explode, burning your hard-earned money.

<u>DO</u> use an iron to get out the wrinkles and make them crisp. But <u>DON'T</u> forget about them or they'll turn extra crispy!

This image makes me cry! Don't worry, Uncle Scrooge, I will NEVER forget about your money!!

DUCKBURG, MY HOME, SWEET HOME

Duckburg has a long and storied history, and most of it involves me. The town started as a fort dating back to the sixteenth century. (It was called Fort Drake Borough by the British and renamed Fort Duckburg during the Revolutionary War.) But things didn't really start hopping till I came along. I decided that Duckburg would be the nerve center of the newly created McDuck Enterprises. It's no exaggeration to say that I put Duckburg on the map!

And speaking of maps, here's a map.

ALL THE AWESOME STUFF ABOUT DUCKBURG SCROOGE LEFT OUT

Let's be honest, he really only left out one awesome thing:

Funso's Funzone . . . where <u>FUN IS IN THE ZONE</u>!!!!!

Webby, you can stop singing now.

BUT I JUST figured out the melody! AND IT. WAS THE GREATEST DAY OF MY LIFE!!!!

INDUSTRIAL DISTRICT

HORNBILL HARBOR

All the Great Things I Did on the GREATEST DAY OF MY LIFE

- Rode a <u>BUS!</u>   And almost got us mugged!

   - Drank PUNCH!
      And lost me my free punch hookup!

- Played a <u>VIDEO GAME!</u>
      It wasn't just a video game, it was a rare
   Japanese import, and the operative word here
   is WAS. . . . You know what? Never mind.

- Escaped a BALL PIT!
                     And captured Ma Beagle,
                        who was trying to kill you.

- Made <u>THREE NEW BEST FRIENDS</u>!!!!!!!

I don't know if the Beagle Boys would call you
their best friend. . . .
                  She means <u>US</u>, Dewey.

SWORN ENEMIES

I've spent decades accumulating my wealth, and along the way I've also accumulated a fair number of foes who foolishly tried to take it away from me.

Flintheart Glomgold—Still trying to get the best of me and still failing miserably.

Magica De Spell— Still no sign of her. Thank heavens.

SWORN ENEMIES (Cont.)

<u>Mark Beaks</u>—Annoys me. I'm annoyed that I'm wasting time even including him. Time is money. Therefore: ENEMY.

<u>Goldie O'Gilt</u>—Ah, Goldie. You know what they say: never trust a hungry thieving jackal to hold your roast. OOOOOooooOOO! SCROOGE'S GIRLFRIEEENND!!!!

Next time you need some gold in your life, come find me! XOXO Always

<u>Percival Threadbare</u>—My old tailor and newest sworn enemy! He suddenly tried to charge me extra for new buttons when they have always been included for free. AND after a mere forty years, he raised his prices by 5 percent—<u>highway robbery!</u>

<u>Ma Beagle and her bumbling boys</u>—I've never been known as a jolly sort, but I do get a particular sense of glee every time one of their ill-conceived plans to break into my money bin goes wrong.

But how did I come up with a money bin? Why don't I follow the crowd and keep my money at the bank? That deserves its own section. Let's see. . . .

<u>Santa Claus</u>—He knows what he did. Keep laughing, old man. I've got my eye on you.

Wait. He's got a beef with SANTA CLAUS?! How's that gonna affect our Christmas?!?!?

My version of Santa Claus.

To an outsider, it might seem foolish to keep all my lovely cash together in a giant money bin. But the wisdom of it becomes clear when you consider my past troubles with other storage methods.

When I was a wee one, I stored all my pennies in a piggy bank. But by the time I was ten, I had a whole herd of piggy banks and had to corral them into a piggy bank pen.

Like my interpretation of Uncle Scrooge's herd of piggy banks??

When I began my money-making career in earnest, I stashed my profits under the mattress. And then under the couch, the easy chair, the kitchen table, and the dining room table and in the freezer. That one gave a whole new meaning to "cold, hard cash." ~~Frozen assets?~~

Soon I discovered the value of secret wall safes and had one installed under a reproduction of the <u>Mona Lisa</u>. Then I had another one put in, and another. Before long, I had approximately thirty copies of the <u>Mona Lisa</u> jammed together on the walls of my office and thought it might look a touch suspicious. Maybe just a touch.

The easiest thing at that point would've been to hand my money over to some well-regarded bank. Well, I don't regard any of them _well_! Bunch of vultures that make their money by holding on to the money of others. There's nary a one of them ever got their hands dirty panning for gold or digging for oil. I'll be buttered and toasted before I let _them_ charge _me_ to store the fortune _I_ fought so hard to build.

So I designed my first money bin. Though technically it would have just been an addition to my existing house. The blueprint was a bit . . . inelegant.

My next money bin plan stood on its own. But the design left a little bit to be desired. I was trying to harken back to the early days of my money-making career but overshot the mark.

All bow before Lord Porkasaurus, lest he open his belly and drown us all in a shower of nickels and dimes!

The third time was the charm! Although it's been rebuilt and reinforced various times, money bin Mach 3 proudly stands in Duckburg to this day!

Love the view from the roof

Wanted a moat filled with crocodiles, but the animal rights people objected

As a compromise, I put it on the shoreline. I chum the water every day to keep sharks <u>in</u> the water and thieves <u>out</u>.

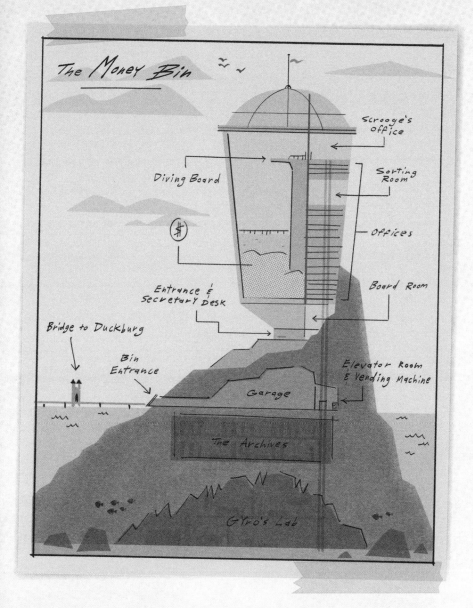

The Money Bin

Scrooge's Office

Sorting Room

Diving Board

Offices

Board Room

Entrance & Secretary Desk

Bridge to Duckburg

Bin Entrance

Elevator Room & Vending Machine

Garage

The Archives

Gyro's Lab

Exterior is reinforced concrete over a layer of steel over a layer of iron over another layer of concrete over a layer of . . . I forget. There are about twenty more layers.

Mastering the Money Pit Dive

1. Stand straight with your shoulders back, tummy tucked in, bottom out, and old-timey full-body swimsuit fastened.

   ←——— Which is surprisingly aerodynamic!

2. Lift your arms straight up, bringing your hands together like you are praying to the sun god Huitzilopochtli. Take a deep breath, allowing the scents of aged metals and the sweat of hard labor to tickle the nostrils. Nope. Louie out.

3. Bend your knees. If one gets stuck, grab your cane and whack your knee until it bends. Good tip! Close your eyes. Nothing stings worse than the ridge of a dime against your cornea.

4. Dive! Allow your hands to lead as you cut through your currenSEA.

5.-8. ENJOY!

KING "LOUIE" THE FIRST

If I'm going to write about the money bin, I'll have to include something about the Beagle Boys' many, many, _many_ attempts to break into it. Actually, it might be fun to mock their ridiculous attempts to steal my money.

Maybe a list of the
<u>Top Ten Silliest Beagle Boy Schemes</u>

1) Dug under the money bin with a giant drill. Ended up striking oil on _my_ property, making me another million.

2) Trained parrots to fly in through the lobby and steal my money, one twenty-dollar bill at a time. I just fed the critters crackers and trained them to say "better luck next time."

3) Used a giant magnet to try to pull all the coins out. Just ended up getting their machine stuck to Audubon Bay Bridge.

4) Snuck a long hose through a window to siphon out the cash like gas from a car. I gave them a mouthful of hornets instead.

5) Tried to melt the money bin with a giant space heater. Just gave themselves a very painful sunburn.

6) Made themselves invisible and snuck inside. When I saw my money floating away on its own, I figured out their scheme. Using long strands of pearls, I swung two feet above the floating money and socked them on their invisible chins.

7) Flooded the money bin and washed my fortune into Mallard Lake, a privately owned body of water. Privately owned . . . by me.

8) Used a giant can opener to peel the top off the money bin. Little did they know that I was using the top floor to store some very rare, very valuable, and very <u>stinky</u> cheeses.

9) Coated the ground with cooking oil to slide the money bin downhill. Ended up slipping and sliding themselves directly into a waiting jail cell.

10) Snuck into my office through the ventilation system and into the vault. They had my money! So I locked them inside with it and told them to eat cash when they got hungry. Three days later, they were paying me $500,000 apiece for some salty pretzels. And a glass of water cost them a cool million.

Ma Beagle

Back to Ma. You can't talk about the Beagle Boys without addressing the most dangerous Beagle of all. I've never seen anyone as adept at using a handbag for a weapon as Ma is.

One thing I've always appreciated about Ma is her loyalty to family. With Ma, family always comes first . . . unless the authorities are involved. Then it's every lad and lassie for themselves.

I've also found that her ability to hold a grudge is second only to mine. Years ago, Grandpappy Beagle stole the deed for Duckburg from the town, renaming it Beagleburg. Never one to miss an opportunity, I conned the deed away from Grandpappy Beagle and graciously returned the town to its previous standing as Duckburg.* Ever since, Ma Beagle has been coming up with ways to steal back the deed to claim what she thinks is "rightfully hers."

*Yeah, but you kept the deed and leased the land to Duckburg citizens, making a profit each month!**

**He's my hero.

So that's Ma Beagle. I wonder if it's worth writing anything more about her seemingly endless "boys"?

Can't see why I should; they all look and act exactly the same. The same grubby sweatshirt and the same silly hat. And the same stupid pea brain! Let's turn the page on this subject. . . .

Wait a minute, Uncle Scrooge! Your info is way out of date. Sure, there's still a group of them who stick to their old style (called the Original Classics). But most of the Beagle Boys have gotten tired of the same old same old and have branched off into various subgroups.

The Glam Yankees—

These guys dress like a 1970s rock band and talk like a bunch of Revolutionary War soldiers. It's a weird combo.

The Glam Yankees

The Déjà Vus—

The costumes are pretty plain and forgettable. But the "forgettable" part is the whole point. They can rob the same bank several times, but they always have the element of surprise, because no one can ever remember their prior robbery. Can't remember where I put their picture.

The Sixth Avenue Meanies—
Rough-and-tumble street
brawlers. They like to hang out in
boxing gyms, dark alleys, and
jail cells. That's not a joke. If
there isn't enough "action" on the
streets, they will get themselves
arrested on purpose so they can
pick a fight in jail.

The Sixth Avenue Meanies

The Sixth Avenue Friendlies—
No one, including the rest of the
Beagle Boys, is quite sure where
these guys came from. They are
super nice. Ridiculously nice. They
spend their time rescuing kittens
from trees and helping senior citizens
cross the street. Our best guess is
that they are playing a "long con"
with some "big score" at the end. But
so far as we can tell, the only plan
the Friendlies have put into action is
working at a soup kitchen five days a
week.

The Sixth Avenue Friendlies

The Longboard Taquitos—
A skateboarding crew that
wasn't good enough to go
pro and turned to crime
instead. I think they also
just really like taquitos.

The Longboard Taquitos

The Tumble Bums—
Eww, just writing their name gives me the creeps. The Bums are a strange troupe of circus performers. They never speak—at least not in any human language. They never walk on two legs. They never fail to give me the shivers.
Avoid at all costs.

The Tumble Bums

The Ugly Failures—
The name says it all, doesn't it? If not, here's a picture.

The Ugly Failures

The Déjà Vus—
The costumes are pretty plain . . . Wait. Did we write about them already?

I don't remember these guys. . . .

Here's something to make the Beagle Boys' mouths water. Read it and weep, boys! You'll never get your grimy mitts on a single nickel!

<u>June 19 Money Bin Coin Breakdown</u>

Pennies---------------------------0
(not worth the space)

Nickels---------------------------7,812,000
(handy for tips)

Plug nickels----------------------20
(handy for vending machines)

Dimes ----------------------------5,437,067

Number One Dime-------------------1

C'mon, Scrooge! We all know you keep your Number One on you at all times. This is an obvious decoy dime.

Like the decoy dime you lost and nearly died trying to get back? THAT kind of OBVIOUS decoy?

I'm never telling you anything again.

<u>June 19 Money Bin Coin Breakdown (CONT.)</u>

Quarters------------------------9,560,336

Silver dollars-------------------8,994,545

Gold doubloons------------------22,560

British shillings----------------12,212

Arcade tokens-------------------15

(keeping them safe for the children)

↑

"Keeping them safe" and charging us rent for storing them.

nother Late-Breaking Addition!!!

The Terrifically Terrifying Tussle with the Terrible Terra-Firmians

"Terrible"?? You liked the Terra-Firmians.

Yes, but good titles always have alliteration.

Sorry, Uncle Scrooge. We would let you take the lead on writing up this adventure, but you were not there! Wait, why wasn't he there?

Because Uncle Scrooge hates the movies and this all started at the movie theater, remember? After the show, you, me, and Lena dropped down into the subway stop in search of the mythical Terra-Firmians.

Lena and I were trying to find them. You thought the whole thing was nonsense.

I was only doubtful because they were not in the Junior Woodchuck Guide. HALLOWED BE ITS NAME.

You scoff, but the JWG has saved us all on numerous occasions!

Like when we needed to learn how to tie a slipknot or find edible tree fungus.

Tree fungus can be very nutritious!!!

Anyways . . . we made our way through the tunnels and along the terrifying train tracks till we—

Did you just learn about alliteration?

We made our way through the tunnels and along the <u>scary rail lines</u> till we came upon an abandoned subway car. It looked as if it had been attacked—

It looked as if it had been <u>stopped</u>. Webby, what are you doing? Why are you trying to make this into a horror movie? You were EXCITED to meet the Terra-Firmians. I was the one who was doubtful and then freaked out when they actually turned out to be real.

I know. I mean—I don't know. I guess I'm just trying to make it sound MOMENTOUS. When we finally got a chance to meet them, they were just cute little rock people.

Seems pretty momentous to me to prove the existence of a "mythical" rock-based life-form.

Awww! What a sweet and yet science-y thing to say.

MYTHICAL CREATURES

The kids seemed surprised to discover that Terra-Firmians actually existed, but not me. Being a world-class adventurer means expecting the unexpected and being prepared to encounter the unencountered.

<u>Arctic Ice Tribe</u>—Took a while to warm up to me. A tragic lesson was learned: never offer tiny people made of ice a cup of hot tea. Hot cocoa is way better.

<u>Leprechauns</u>—Sneaky lads not to be trusted. I once accidentally found myself on the wrong side of a rainbow. After I snatched their pot of gold, they tried to get me to invest it in a promising new venture, then laughed at my spats.

Regular rainbows are way overrated.

<u>Werewolves</u>—
Everyone's SO AFRAID of werewolves. They're just little furry death puppies! Defeat a whole pack, and you have yourself a handsome profit once you auction them off to Iditarod teams.

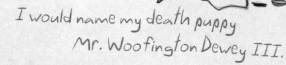

I would name my death puppy Mr. Woofington Dewey III.

<u>Unicorns</u>—Ack. "Sword horses." Silly creatures with an overrated horn who have, I must admit, a very keen instinct for stock picking (though they do consistently undervalue McDuck Enterprises).

EEEE!!! SWORD HORSES!!!

<u>Toadstools</u>—Often mistaken for mushrooms. To eat them guarantees death. At night, these mythical beings hop around like frogs, and each croaks one distinct word. If you can get them to croak in the right order, the resulting sentence will lead to a great treasure. Worth the wait from a financial perspective.

<u>Sirens</u>—Creatures with the unnerving talent of mind-controlling song. There's an old adventuring bachelor joke: What's worse, a child or a siren? Everyone laughs, because they are both awful.

That's not a nice joke.

I don't get it.

<u>Vampires</u>—The standard bloodsucking ones are a dime a dozen these days, but I had an encounter with a rarer type that's worth a page or three. . . .

What do you call a dozen dimes?

A dollar twenty? Actually, yes. Lame.

Why did he put "sword horses" in quotation marks? Has he <u>no respect</u> for their majesty?! Their BEAUTIFUL, <u>DEADLY</u> MAJESTY??? They glide like the wind, their horns slicing through flesh like hot knives through butter. They—Hey, why are you guys backing away from me?

CHAPTER TWO:
That Time I Took Out a Luck Vampire

Everybody's such nervous Nellies when it comes to vampires. "Oh, they possess eternal life." "Oh, they feast on blood/luck/happiness/etc." "Oh, they wear creepy capes." A bunch of boo-hoo. Defeating vampires is easy. The thing you have to remember about vampires is that they aren't smart; they aren't clever; but they sure are LITERAL. Words and what you say are everything to a vampire. So don't ramble, be concise, and think about how you can really stick it to them.

Gladstone Gander is a member of my family who's known for being lucky, and he is astonishingly lazy because of it.

(For further explanation/ranting, see LAZY FAMILY on Page 50.)

The ancient luck vampire Liu Hai took Gladstone captive to feast on his luck. Instead of making his own way and saving himself, the dallying loafer decided to call on me to save him. I rallied Donald and the children, and off we went to save his feathers. But what he and Liu Hai weren't banking on was that luck didn't make me the wealthy trillionaire I am today. It was smarts! Determination! Pure Scottish grit!

Umm, you didn't do all that much, Uncle Scrooge.

It wasn't even that scary.

I just remember being really impressed with Uncle Donald. Because that doesn't happen often.

Liu Hai challenged me to an obstacle course, taking two of my family members hostage to run his gauntlet. The winner would be granted their freedom. Thinking he was clever, the vampire chose my nephew Donald as my gladiator, while Gladstone served as his. Everyone knew that in a race between Donald and Gladstone, the unlucky hotheaded nephew of mine was at a severe disadvantage. But Donald's rage improbably allowed him to win the race and it seemed like Gladstone was doomed.

Places I would take Dewey Jr.:
The mall, Funzo's, EVERYWHERE

While the race would secure the freedom of one fortunate individual, it didn't properly defeat Liu Hai. That's where I relied on my smarts. Having Donald best Gladstone proved that he, not Gladstone, was indeed the luckiest guy on Earth. Liu Hai bit the bait, so to speak . . . and choked when Donald's bad luck caused him to starve, defeating him forever . . . or until the next time he shows up. Pesky vampires don't stay dead. I'll always remember you, Dewey Jr.

While the incident didn't show off my physical skill or prowess, it did cement my ability to be a formidable foe in all things logic and reason.

Lazy Family

This ought to be good.

Should we read this? Do we really want to know where we stand with Uncle Scrooge?

As in the order of his will? YES. ABSOLUTELY.

OOOH!!! Constructive criticism! Yay!

Gladstone gets by in life because of one thing: he is lucky. I don't like it. It's like I always say: luck is for ducks with no pluck. If I had Gladstone's luck, combined with my tenacity, work ethic, charm, and good looks, there'd be nothing I couldn't do. I'll admit, I have my issues with Donald, but I'll take that hotheaded bag of jinx over that freeloading layabout Gladstone any day of the week. And that's as soft as I get.

I have more to write in this section, but for now I'll take a break. Where's me tea?

Possible Daft Duck album title.

Phew! He didn't even mention us.

Boo!

Wait. I want to make a few notes about the kids.
I spoke too soon.

But we're not lazy! Well, Louie kinda is.

I'm not lazy, I'm conserving my energy.

HUEY:

I am starting to see just how valuable this one is. . . . But I'm still not fully convinced. He's way too literal. And he's always with that book. I'm all for learning, but sooner or later you've got to cast the book aside and take a chance.

OH, WOW!

What is he even talking about, "too literal"? Also, I would NEVER throw my Junior Woodchuck Guide aside! That is a book that must be handled WITH CARE.

Yeah, he's way off base.

DEWEY:

A stubborn old gander of a boy. Tenacious, like a mule. Hardheaded at all the wrong times.

I'm hardheaded?

I'M hardheaded???

He's one to talk!

Dewey Junior!

LOUIE:

Still "impressed" by this one's complete lack of ambition. A blobfish is more motivated.

Can't argue with that.

WEBBIGAIL:

Not a member of the family, but sometimes I wish she were. Her grandmother has taught her well. She's got the skills of a first-class adventurer.

I think I might faint!!

What she doesn't have is the skills of an everyday child. Has Beakley been keeping her in a box when she isn't training her?

Ouch! I wish I <u>had</u> fainted instead of reading that last part.

Time to draw things that make me feel happy!

CHAPTER THREE:
Unwrapping the Mummies of Toth-Ra

Finding the lost tomb of Toth-Ra was no easy feat. The tomb had everything I was expecting (treasure, booby traps, quicksand) and a few things I wasn't (living mummies). When the wee bairns Webby and Louie disappeared from the group, I knew I had to do the honorable (and legally sound) thing and find them before I went looking for the treasure. But I also knew I couldn't do it alone. Luckily, I had a small rebel army of mummies willing to rise up against the Pharaoh in the name of burritos. (A gift more precious than sunlight, apparently. Personally, I don't get the appeal!)

Yeah, where did Louie and Webby go?

Treasure doesn't find itself, guys.

WE HAD THE MOST EPIC ADVENTURE!

Webby, play it cool.

Cool. Okay. Sooooooooooo, like, don't recap our mummy adventure in haiku on the next page?

If there's a bunch of haikus on the next page, I'm going to be very upset.

You might want to skip the next page, then.

WEBBY AND LOUIE'S PYRAMID ADVENTURE!
IN HAIKU!

I MIGHT EVEN ADD IAMBIC PENTAMETER LATER!

Together we slide
Through the great lost pyramid
But split from the group.

A room of treasure!
Many wonderful delights!
Rare gemstones! Kidneys!

Nearly killed by spikes
We found a secret passage
To the great Toth-Ra!

But he was a fake.
Then the real Toth-Ra woke up!
It was such a mess.

The sun shone brightly
As we rolled a burrito
Chock-full of mummy.

Quesadillas, please!
This place is so delicious.
I really love cheese.

This . . . is shockingly impressive.

"Single-handedly" is a stretch when we were with you THE WHOLE TIME!!!

I (single-handedly) rallied the rebellion of mummies against their grubby, gold-grabbing leader, surprising even myself with my inspiring cries for freedom. But if there's one thing I've always believed in, it's the ability of one to think and act for him—or herself, to make one's own way free of the shackles of tyranny. No leader's gonna take my hard-earned loot! As a wee lad, I earned my lucky dime with work and sweat. I answered to no one but myself, and these living mummies deserved the same freedoms. We soon learned that the "Pharaoh" was simply a guard who was scaring the mummies into submission, and it seemed all was fine . . . until the prophecy was fulfilled and a horrible demonic mummy sprang to life and tried to kill us all, as they do.

I led the group to take on the terrifying Pharaoh Toth-Ra by wrapping him tightly in a blanket, a technique I picked up on one of my many adventures.

Hey! That was OUR idea!!!

It was truly an adventure for the ages, as I was able to teach the young ones that some things, like freedom, are more precious than gold. And I'm not just saying that because Launchpad was gifted gold and I was gifted a burrito. I'm not.

Sidenote: How to Stretch a Penny—
Cheap Places to Eat

Lessons learned on how to save money eating out so you have more money in the vault . . .

-Must have daily specials. Every restaurant has something they are trying to pawn off on customers before it expires. I'll take it, but not before bargaining down the price first. Everything's negotiable.

-Free refills on beverages while you eat. I've found if you bring an extra top hat, place it atop an old burlap sack stuffed with napkins, then leave it in a booth while you go about your day, you can come back for drink refills and no one will be the wiser.

He is so wise.

-Two-for-one specials. Bonus if you can fit the extra food in your pocket for later.

-Day-old pastries. Who needs soft baked goods? I like my scones tough enough to double as a formidable weapon if needed.

NOT that taco truck in Egypt. Avoid that place.

CHAPTER FOUR:
That Time I Climbed Mount Neverrest

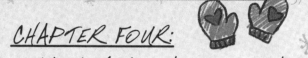

After these first few adventures, I was feeling warmed up enough to make some history. So I decided to become . . .

the first duck to climb to the peak of Mount Neverrest!

I had not spied the mountain for seventy-five years, but upon my arrival, the memories of my earlier attempt flooded over me. Unfortunately, a group of hucksters selling T-shirts and postcards also flooded over me. It seemed that a tourist trap village had sprung up around the base of Neverrest.

I fought my way past the snow-globe kiosks and hot dog vendors and finally made it to the base of the mountain. George Mallardy had begun his fateful ascent seventy-five years earlier from the very same spot. He had climbed higher up Mount Neverrest than any duck before or after. And I was going to beat the pants off his ridiculous old record, even if it killed me.

And it nearly did! Turns out that it's impossible to reach the summit of Neverrest. Silly peak has a bunch of mystical dimensional portals protecting it. You're within arm's reach of the top, and with the next step up— SHZZZOOPP—you suddenly find yourself one thousand feet lower. I tried all afternoon to find the right combination of "holes" to get me to the top, but you'd have better luck traversing a piece of Swiss cheese.

I climbed higher up the mountain than Mallardy, but I was not destined to reach the top. With the sun setting, I decided the safest thing was to give up. I treated my nephew Huey to a sled ride down the mountain.

C'mon, Uncle Scrooge!

<u>I'M</u> the one who convinced <u>you</u> to give up on the summit. <u>I'M</u> the one who figured out the whole wormhole thing. And I'm <u>NOT</u> the one who was into sledding. The whole sledding thing was Webby and Dewey's deal.

And what a SWEET deal it was!!

I now realize how incomplete my life has been without sledding in it. When can we go again? How about tomorrow?

That reminds me—I <u>still</u> have not gotten repaid for all the junk Launchpad and Louie bought in that silly village at the base of the mountain.

<u>Launchpad's Expenses:</u>

Safety pamphlet about the "deadly ice fever"	$10.99
Triple-fur-lined parka	$139.99
Fever-Go-Way heat-generating cream	$12.59
Combination thermometer/heart rate monitor/mood ring	$225.50
Oxygen tank rental to stop "fever vision"	$75.01
12 pairs of thermal socks (12?)	$62.35
12 pairs of thermal gloves (Again—12??)	$89.95
"Commemorative" ice fever canteen	$35.25
TOTAL	I'M TOO ANGRY TO DO MATH!!!

I've never had someone spend so much of my money to combat a made-up disease. And if "ice fever" was a real thing, why would you buy a canteen to commemorate it??? As absurd as Launchpad's expenses were, at least he kept track of them. Here's what I got from Louie:

Essentials @ $25-$500

"Essentials"? Really? I could survive for a week on Mount Neverrest with only a can of tuna and a matchbook, but everything he spots is "essential." That boy needs to learn the value of a dollar!

That's unfair. I know the value of a dollar! It's 99 cents, give or take a few pennies. And everything I purchased at Neverrest was essential to me having a good time!! Take a look:

Double-Dark Scorching-Hot Hot Chocolate to warm my belly

Iced Chocoloccino to soothe my burnt tongue (They're not kidding about "scorching.")

Fur-lined snowshoes with 100 percent real yeti fur (the lushest of cryptid furs)

One-year membership to the Neverrest Never Worry Spa and Hot Springs (For only twice the cost of a day pass, you get 365-day access! This is just good economics.)

Neverrest
Never Worry
spa and hot springs

1 - Year
Membership Card

I could go on and on, but I think I've made my point.

I suppose I can't be boasting about my survival skills in my autobiography unless I include a few tips to back up my claims.

Survival Skills for the Coldest Spots on Earth

<u>Problem</u>—The temperature is dropping and your coat is as thin as a tissue.

<u>Solution</u>—Throw your coat away and make a parka out of your greenbacks. Nothing keeps a duck warmer than snuggling up next to his money.

<u>Problem</u>—The snow is too soft and you keep sinking into it.

<u>Solution</u>—Make snowshoes out of your checkbooks.

<u>Problem</u>—You're attacked by a polar bear.

<u>Solution</u>—Pack your spare change into the middle of snowballs and throw them at the beast. Don't forget to collect the coins after the fight is over.

I suggest we rip this page out before giving the notebook back to Uncle Scrooge.

<u>Problem</u>—You encounter the Abominable Snowman.
<u>Solution</u>—This is no problem at all! The Abominable Snowman (or Archibald, as he prefers to be called) is a wonderful fellow. Sure, he may look a little rough around the edges, but if you are stuck in the frozen wilderness, there's no one better to stumble across than good ol' Archie!

If you stumble across some penguins, stumble back the other way. Nasty little beasts with no manners, despite the fact that they "dress" in tuxedos.

I first met Archie back in '52 when I was searching for oil near the Arctic Circle. I was going around in a circle after I lost my way in a sudden snowstorm. Luckily for me, Archie was out in the storm, walking his pet walrus.

He offered me shelter in his "man cave," which was, of course, an actual cave. Despite that, it was a most comfortable evening with a very gracious host. The furnishings reflected a familiarity with international culture. Archie is a well-traveled fellow who can visit any part of the globe undetected as long as there is some snowfall to provide cover. However, most of the time he sticks to the less populated poles. He likes to "winter" in the Arctic and then "winter" in Antarctica, as well.

<u>Note to self:</u> Try to get a better picture of Archie before publication. Bleedin' snowstorms seem to ruin every photo!

Speaking of survival skills, should I write about all the ways I've made money in the frozen North? There was that small business I had charging tourists to see the northern lights.

Maybe my next autobiography . . .

NO! NO!! NO!!!!!

Why does he stop every time he gets to the good stuff?? How am I going to make my fortune if he won't tell me how he made his fortune?!!!

I suppose he expects me to "work harder and smarter than everyone else," like he did. Just a couple of small problems with that plan: the words "hard" and "work."

Kids these days need tutoring in skills they aren't learning from the telly. Important lessons are to be learned. I'm going to create a section called SCROOGE'S SCRAMBLINGS and impart wisdom for which, frankly, I should be charging them. Wait, why am I doing this, again? Yes, why ARE you doing this when you could be giving us tips on getting RICH?

This sounds BOOOOOORING. ARGH!! And I've learned great things from TV! Like how to build an ottoman! Ooo, I can't wait!

How to draw a perfect bath:

Turn off the hot-water spigot and run the cold water from the tap. If you are smart and cheap, you will have one small water heater to supply the entire mansion so guests don't run up your water and electricity bills luxuriating in hot-water baths and showers and the like. The cold from the tap is plenty warm. When I used to bathe in the Klondike, my baths were colder than a polar bear's drool, and I was able to relax just fine. It's all about stamina and grit.   Noted!

Fill tub to one plume past your belly. Not a plume more! Got it!

Don't bother with soap. The cost-effectiveness is minimal and it ruins the water. Who knew?!

When finished, run bathwater through a sieve and reuse. I like to get at least three to five baths from one tub.

Fascinating. Thanks for all that! My next three to five baths are going to be sensational!

If you really wanted to save money, you'd just cannonball into your pool, which is already filled. YOU'RE WELCOME, Uncle Scrooge.

Well, the day I was dreading—my birthday—has come and gone. I thought I had successfully scared everyone I knew into not mentioning the awful event, but I had forgotten one thing. Or rather, _three_ things . . .

My nephews.

The scamps had the unmitigated gall to throw me a birthday _party_!!! Can you imagine?!

Huey was, of course, the organizer. Nothing says "spontaneous celebration" like a twelve-point checklist of mandatory activities. Though I have to admit that as far as horribly painful experiences go, it wasn't all bad.

I'll take it!! From Scrooge, "not all bad" is a ringing endorsement of my party-planning skills!

Let's weigh the pros and cons.

CONS

Boring birthday games

Dewey doing some weird robot-musician thing

Substandard snack food   Some GREAT weird robot-musician thing!

Guest list was 100 percent archvillains, thanks to Louie and his 0 percent effort.

Worst of all—a magician!   Is it my fault that the rich and powerful of Duckburg also happen to be the evil and insane of Duckburg??

PROS

Got to fake my own disappearance and possible death

Mental anguish inflicted on villains and family

Got my favorite butler, Duckworth, returned to my service

Having Duckworth around is driving Beakley crazy.

ADDITIONAL CON

Duckworth is a ghost, so he can't really do any heavy lifting.

Never understood why anyone would celebrate their birthday. What's there to celebrate? The accomplishment of being born? I prefer to celebrate _Worthdays_ (patent pending).

A Worthday is the day on which I reach a new milestone in my net worth.

Past celebrations include:

Worth a million—bought myself a new tie[*]

Worth a billion—bought myself a second hat

Worth a trillion—took a two-hour lunch break (made up the time the next day)

Worth a quadrillion—tried to get the treasury department to issue a quadrillion-dollar bill to eliminate the storage costs of my vast fortune

Worth an incredibillion—built a new, improved, larger money bin. Tried to pay the builder in cash, but the guy couldn't break a quadrillion-dollar bill.

So don't be expecting a present from me until you hit your first million.

You're just trying to get out of wearing a party hat.

[*]Uncle Scrooge told us he celebrated his first million with his first climb up Mount Neverrest. Is he lying here to cover up the whole "Neverrest Ninny" thing?

~~OR is there something bigger going on??? A whole series of lies and fake histories that will ultimately lead to~~

CHAPTER FIVE:
Winning the Links of Moorshire

Let us take a moment here, a small pause, to honor the great sport of the ages: golf. "Oh, but Mr. McDuck," you're whining, "there's not enough cheering! There's not enough fan gear! There are no air horns!" *There's really not.*

THAT'S RIGHT! I like my sport with intense focus and polite clapping, not filled with screams in the air like your kilt's on fire. Golf is a game that requires patience, logic, and emotional restraint. It should come as no surprise to anyone that this Scotsman is one of the *second* greatest players in the world.

Moorshire is the birthplace of golf and one of the greatest courses on Earth. And like all great places on Earth, there is more to this course than meets the eye.

I had the great honor of playing one of the world's worst golfers (and my personal archnemesis), Flintheart Glomgold, at the Duckburg Billionaires' Club Golf Invitational, held at the Links of Moorshire. Glomgold is so bad it is comical, and yet it was I who found my ball slicing into the misty woods.

Reader, let me warn you now: when you see a circle of Celtic standing stones, use your noggin and don't walk in the middle of the circle. You are asking for trouble. Or adventure. Strike that; when you see a circle of Celtic standing stones, ALWAYS WALK RIGHT INTO IT. If there's a weird glowing light, <u>EVEN BETTER.</u>

THIS IS TERRIBLE ADVICE. YOU SHOULD <u>ALWAYS</u> RUN!!!

Being a Scotsman, I always play where my ball lands, <u>even</u> if it lands in a circle of Celtic standing stones. This time, as I tried to swing my way out of the circle, we were all teleported to a faerie

realm, where we were greeted by two tiny ponies. But these weren't just any ponies; they were kelpies, nasty creatures who tempt innocent souls onto their backs so they can carry them off into the sea! (<u>Note to self</u>: add KELPIES to Mythical Creatures list.) It was clear to me that these kelpies were out for us when they challenged us to play the ancient course in order to get back to our realm.

I identified the kelpies, thank you very much! I love a tiny pony, especially if it's trying to drown me.

A golfer must always think strategically above all else, and I knew these surly Shetlands weren't fooling around. The Druids took their golf very seriously. There would be traps unlike any I'd seen before. There would be natural hazards that would place the odds against us. So I did what any good player would do: let Glomgold play through first. While Flinty set off the traps, I, and I alone, worked my way through the course, hole by hole. Alone? If it wasn't for me, you'd still be golfing in another realm!

At the final hole, the mists started rolling in . . . turning Glomgold to stone and threatening to turn me next! I took a pause and watched as the rolling mists started to turn everyone I loved to stone. WAIT. Did he just say he loved us?

I realized the strategic move would be to let someone a wee bit brash take their turn, so I handed my club to Dewey. I knew it'd be an important life lesson . . . because our lives were at stake! With me as a mentor, the lad took the most important shot of his life and clinched it! Soon we were back in our realm, safe and sound.

My trip to Moorshire (and my latest encounter with Glomgold) has reminded me how much I love to insult fools in Scots.

Favorite Scottish Insults

bampot—idiot

boggin—foul-smelling

clipe—tattletale

doaty dobber—simple idiot

eejit—idiot

feartie—coward

gommy—idiot

gowk—fool, idiot

numpty—idiot

roaster—idiot

talking mince—talking rubbish

tube—idiot

Who knew there were so many words for "idiot"?

Don't be such a doaty dobber, you boggin mince-talking gommy gowk.

I'm gonna need a sec to translate that.

HEY!!!

CHAPTER SIX:
The Return to Ithaquack

Reader, it should be known that the gods don't like to be bested. We mortals are way more relaxed about that sort of thing. The gods hold on to grudges forever. I was reminded of this when that hapless sack of piloting skills Launchpad crashed us into Ithaquack, an island I'd been banned from by the god Zeus because I was better than him. And smarter than him. And could build a better sand castle than him. Needless to say, I wasn't surprised when he trapped us all on the island and held a contest to see whose family—mine or his—was better at heroic trials.

I know the answer's obvious, but indulge me.

A picture of "Hubert, Tamer of Winds, and ~~Llywelyn~~ Fighter of Storms."

Webby!

Claiming Aeolus's bag of winds involved smarts, not just strength. Sailing across and over the winds, as I suggested, gave the red-shirted lad Huey a single-handed victory.* A discus throw proved that Donald's approach, apathy, was indeed the approach to take. We bested Zeus's family in chariot racing, clay sculpting, and being mean (stealing** the Golden Fleece from a small child), but we ultimately proved to be too trusting when it was revealed that the small child was actually a siren (see MYTHICAL CREATURES, pages 45-46). The siren brainwashed our friend Storkules, and he came forward to murder us. Donald stepped in to create a distraction, and I defeated the hypnotized bird AND stopped the horrid siren song!

WHOA WHOA WHOA. I offered to be her talent manager and she agreed. That siren had some pipes!

*What?? That was totally MY idea, thanks to my Junior Woodchuck Sailing Badge. →

**Me "being mean" won us the fleece, didn't it? Having your toys snatched is part of being a kid. No big deal.

But I knew Zeus would not rest until I was properly defeated, so I threw a game of bocce.
And that, Reader, is the only time on record Scrooge McDuck has ever been beaten at anything. EVER. <u>EVER.</u>

THINGS I AM BETTER AT THAN ZEUS

Beach volleyball

Building sand castles

Limbo

Tongue twisters

Finding treasure

Killing unkillable creatures

Dewey and Webby,
you guys are being awfully quiet over there.

Who, US? Heh heh, no reason! No reason at all! We had a great time at Ithaquack! So much to do . . . and see . . . that has nothing to do with uncovering secrets or finding hidden artifacts that directly relate to

WEBBY!!!

All this gallivanting across the globe is proving detrimental to my bottom line! There was at least 75-80 cents that I could not account for at the end of last week. Going to need to track my budget more closely.

Daily Spending — Wednesday the 25th

$.05	Nickel lost when flipping a coin to see what kind of tea I'd have: Scottish Breakfast or Tranquil Moments. Settled on Nutmeg, as always.
$1.25	Morning financial paper
-$1.25	Return of money when I realize I own the paper
$2.68	LUNCH: day-old hunk of bread, the perfectly good cheese rind the cafeteria worker was just going to throw out, and cup of hot water to reuse tea bag from morning
-$.30	Return of money when I pointed out not-so-quietly that I brought my own mug for the hot water
$5.00	Bet I lost to Dewey (Don't ask.)
$10.00	Payoff money to Huey and Louie so they wouldn't tell anyone I lost said bet to Dewey

Just got back from a fun little race/near-fatal car crash between Launchpad and this newfangled robot-driven jalopy. Based on this latest encounter with an evil robot, I'd have to say that the promise of automated automobiles is still a ways off. And I, for one, am happy to hear it!

I've always felt that a duck should be the driver of his own destiny. And of his own car, boat, plane, or whatever else he chooses to get him where he needs to be! Yes, I do let Launchpad do a lot of the driving these days, but that's only because I've logged more than my share of miles in past years.

Perhaps a section on my most famous races would make sense. . . .

Blathering blatherskite!

MY MOST FAMOUS RACES

<u>The Monte Carlo Rally</u>—The history books say that this annual auto race was started by Albert I, the prince of Monaco, and I suppose in a way that's true. Al loved to gamble but hated paying up when he lost. He owed a sizable chunk of change to me and a dozen other business professionals all over Europe. When I heard that the globe-trotting prince was back home to make another withdrawal from the Royal Bank, I "rallied" all his creditors and we "raced" toward Monte Carlo to collect.

<u>Scrooge's Cup</u>—The New York Yacht Club refused my yacht's entrance into the America's Cup, saying that only yacht <u>CLUBS</u>, not single yachts, could compete. To show up those snobs, I started my own race, called Scrooge's Cup. Any sailing vessels could enter for a chance to win the trophy (the trophy being the porcelain "sippy cup" I had used as a toddler). Remarkably, no one else decided to compete.

<u>Trans-Atlantic Air Derby</u>—Few remember that Charles Lindbergh's historic flight from New York to Paris was inspired by a cash prize of $25,000. I was after that money, as well, and fully intended to beat "Lucky Lindy" in a race to Paris. I became known as "Unlucky McDucky" after my plane blew up on the runway. I had substituted expensive airplane fuel with more cost-effective Appalachian moonshine.

<u>The First Tour de France</u>—I fell into this bike race by accident while spending an infuriatingly lazy Sunday afternoon on a bicycle built for two. When the racers sped by, my natural competitive temperament compelled me to join in. I finished the day in the top five!

I also finished off my chances at a second date with the young lass who had been riding the bike with me.

Ooooh! Scrooge didn't talk about <u>any</u> of these races in his first autobiography! And who's this mysterious beauty on the bike?? Was she one of Scrooge's early loves???

It says right here they never had a second date.

Too late. I'm already writing fanfic.

The Young Duck and the Sea of Money—
A Dewey Duck Adventure

The sea is a funny and fickle mistress. And my uncle Scrooge's sea of money is just as faithless as any body of water. I could only pray that luck would be with me as I set sail inside the money bin in search of a most awesome foe— the legendary money shark. (Or maybe "Jaw$"? We'll workshop the name.)

This beast had already taken my two dear brothers, the helpless maidens Webbigail and Lena, and my even more helpless best friend, Launchpad. It was up to me, and me alone, to stop him.

I suddenly spotted my foe! He was dead ahead of me and

What the heck is this??!! You weren't the last duck standing. You were the **FIRST** to get eaten!!

YEAH! And it was the "helpless maidens" Webby and Lena who saved you. Though to be fair, we were also eaten before we did the saving. ♥

 Hey, if Uncle Scrooge is going to fudge the details and make things up, I don't see why I can't do the same.

♥ That's an awful lot of "fudging the details" in just a few sentences.

Why is everyone writing about fudge? Did somebody make fudge? Did you guys eat all the fudge already??? ♥

SO . . . there was a crazy magical money shark thing that was made out of money and fed on money. But it also liked to feed on us. DEWEY got swallowed FIRST, followed by Launchpad and the other boys and then Lena and me, but Lena and I defeated it with the MAGIC POWER OF FRIENDSHIP!

The truth is dorky. My story was cool.

CHAPTER SEVEN:
That Time I Found Liquid Gold
(and Subsequently Lost It)

ahhhhhhh, what? →

And he also fell in LOVE!

Gross.

While I've spent my life a confirmed bachelor, namely for tax reasons, that doesn't mean I haven't found myself under the spell of someone. But not just <u>any</u> someone—the only individual in the world who could come close to besting me.

Sure, that's it.

OH, Goldie O'Gilt! I read all about her in Uncle Scrooge's unauthorized biography.

I still have hives from that awful suit.

But first, let's talk about relationships these days. Young ones are content to have a meal and declare devotion. Phooey! You want the devotion of Scrooge McDuck, you have to earn it! You have to show keen wit and prowess. Bravery in the face of pure cursed evil.

True love doesn't waste money on plant life that's only gonna die, sucking down YOUR water in a vessel YOU provide. Is he talking about . . . flowers?

True love leaves you for dead in the Gobi Desert! True love sells you to Portuguese pirates and throws you out of an airship over the Himalayas. True love leaves you in a glacier when the sun's rays thaw it out after five long years of your being frozen together!

Goldie O'Gilt is my ex in every sense of the word, but she's the only one who figured out how to get under my skin.

EWWW!

OOooOOooh!

They say love will keep you young. They also say age is just a state of mind.

"They" are full of sentimental hogwash.

REAL WAYS TO STAY YOUNG

- Fountain of Youth. The one in Wronguay is easiest/cheapest to reach.

- Timeless demon dimensions always have a charm or two to keep you immortal. Demogorgona has the Eye of Demogorgon. Pandemonium has the Infernal Sword. Both have demons who are soooo sensitive. Pit them against each other for a distraction and grab that loot.

- Win a bet against Old Man Time. For all the fussing he does with minutes, he's terrible at math. Use this to your advantage.

- Fall into a glacier and freeze. It helps if you have something nice to look at, like a stack of gold bars or blue-chip stock certificates.

- Walk backwards against the Earth's rotation. Not recommended on islands or mountaintops.

How old IS Uncle Scrooge?

Well, if he's done all of these things, he's probably close to a thousand years old, give or take a few decades. That's scientifically impossible.

That's right. And vampires are imaginary.

Well— And there's no such thing as a faerie realm.

Okay, but— I rest my case.

Goldie and I have lived many lives, and they've always run parallel to each other. Sometimes they've merged like conglomerates; sometimes they've parted like an FCC shakeup. But always in the back of my mind, ~~like a lost penny~~ (bad analogy, I never lose pennies), there's glittering Goldie.

I hadn't seen Goldie for a number of years, so at first my memory was a bit foggy when I caught a glimpse of her at Flintheart Glomgold's museum opening. I had pockets full of shrimp puffs and eyes full of stars. Then the sound of a dropped catering tray brought me back to reality, and I remembered what to do when Goldie O'Gilt is in your midst: RUN! Blame Dewey!

Hey!

SOME GOLD-SEEKING ADVENTURES WITH GOLDIE

<u>Dawson Days:</u>
She was the proprietor of the Blackjack Saloon, and I was an old sourdough making my way to the Klondike to find my fortune.

Escaping the Bermuda Triangle:
In our quest for sunken treasure, she sailed us out of the reach of giant octopi and got us to solid ground with our trunks of treasure by day's end, without a single piece lost.

Granny and I can attest: she's really good with knots.

Golden Lagoon of White Agony Plains (twice):
We searched for the legendary lagoon made of liquid gold. Best encounter with an unfrozen woolly mammoth I've seen to date.

Putting on Airs at Ayers Rock:
We got word there was a vein of gold deep in the landmark protected by killer kangaroos. When they had us cornered, she figured out a way to saddle them and leap us to safety.

Goldie O'Gilt is one of the few who knew me before I was the world's richest duck, and I suppose that's why I have such a soft spot for that no-good backstabbing greedy grifter.

It doesn't sound like he's over her.

It sounds to me like true love!

It sounds to me like Uncle Scrooge is losing focus. This does NOT bode well for my inheritance.

When Glomgold unveiled the skull of the Glacier Monster of the Klondike, a woolly mammoth that had lived through the Ice Age and beyond, I realized why Goldie had come around.

We had met that beast before, she and I.

In our younger days, we had set out to find the Golden Lagoon of White Agony Plains, a river made of pure liquid gold, using a map I had acquired. But that swindling minx stole my map! As I chased her down, we encountered the hideous beast, who ate half the map. The Glacier Monster wasn't found again until Glomgold's oil expedition uncovered a lot more than oil. Goldie was there to snatch the map back! I, of course, still had the other half of the map, locked up in a VERY safe place.

Eh, it was in your top hat, next to the bunny and the flock of doves (haha).

Because of our history, I knew if I wanted to find the Golden Lagoon of White Agony Plains, it meant teaming up with her. Only one other being on this Earth loves gold more than I do, so much so it's in her name.**

Uh, what about GlomGOLD? Also, has Uncle Scrooge ever met Louie?

**Although, it's in that right fool Glomgold's name as well. ACK. Mental note: revise this section and cut the sentimental malarkey.

So after a long talk, off we went to find the one treasure that had eluded me. . . .

Where she broke into the mansion. . . .

And tied me and Granny up!

And stole his hat!

I don't remember much of a talk.

THE GOLDEN LAGOON OF WHITE AGONY PLAINS!!!

We traveled deep underground, through a series of caverns, and ice, and ice caverns. An elevator led us to the Rainbow Caves. We knew we were close! But little did we know, my mortal enemy Flintheart Glomgold had followed us!

okay, what to write next? Hmmmmm . . .

(NOTE TO SELF: revise these pages.)

I took a moment to meet up with an old friend,
Nanook the grizzly bear.

Wait—you stopped searching for treasure to
meet up with a friend? That doesn't sound right.

Adventure IS his friend!
And Danger is his business
partner!

REALLY, Webby?

We passed Mammoth Mesa, ~~where Goldie and~~ Hey, why
~~I were once frozen in ice together years~~ ← is this
~~earlier,~~ and heard the sound of water on crossed
the other side of a thin wall of ice. With out?
the help of my friend Nanook, we burst
through the wall and discovered the lagoon!

THINGS YOU CAN DO WITH LIQUID GOLD

-Fix broken dishes

-Dip worthless items in it and gold-plate them to increase resale value

-Put it in a squirt gun and play Medusa for the afternoon. Loads of fun! Just don't spray anyone in the eye.

-Spread it on a sandwich for a funny joke. Liquid gold is often mistaken for mustard. Just don't actually eat it. It will singe your insides.

THINGS YOU CAN'T DO WITH LIQUID GOLD

-Swim in it. It will burn you alive.

-Drink it. It will burn you from the inside out.

-Touch it. It will scorch you.

-Breathe it in. It will infuse your entire respiratory system with gold and you'll get a case of "prospector wheeze."

-Look at it for too long. It will blind you.

It was great finding the Golden Lagoon, the one treasure that had eluded me, after all those years. But while I was down there, I decided that I had enough gold for one duck, and it would be better to share. *Wait, what?* WHAT?

At that point, Glomgold had caught up with us, so I shook his hand and left, allowing him and Goldie to decide the fate of all that liquid gold. THE END. MOVING ON. WHAT?!

NOOOOOOOOOOOOOOOOO...

Something feels off about this story.
I needed Nanook closure.

CHAPTER EIGHT:
That Time I Had to Save Beakley

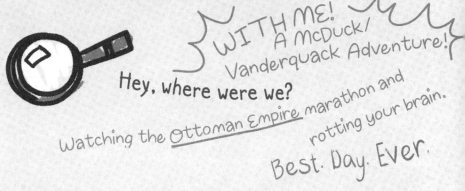

WITH ME! A McDuck/ Vanderquack Adventure!

Hey, where were we?

Watching the <u>Ottoman Empire</u> marathon and rotting your brain.

Best. Day. Ever.

Many of you out there don't know the history of Beakley and me. Yes, she is my most trusted confidante. Yes, she makes a perfect cup of tea. Yes, the two are not mutually exclusive.

Acronyms from our past:

F.O.W.L. —Fiendish Organization for World Larceny

S.H.U.S.H. —???

What does "S.H.U.S.H." stand for?

It's an acronym so secret nobody actually knows!

I'd be impressed if I wasn't so annoyed.

In 1968, I was a handsome duck-about-town, dazzling all of Swinging London with my charm, my wit, and my natural ability to pull off a derby. One day, I was approached by the secret organization S.H.U.S.H. and tasked with a mission: infiltrate the exclusive auction of Bonbon & Buttermilk with Agent 22, who was none other than . . . Beakley!

Beakley was a spy???? This explains so much.

I was a freelance spy in those days, in it for the cool gadgets.

WAIT, YOU WERE A SPY, TOO???

Gadgets???? There's a Junior Woodchuck badge all about making gadgets! If only you had included a diagram that I could follow to build one myself. . . .

Nice hat, haha.

JACKPOT!

Instant-film camera—
You never know when
a camera will prove
useful.

Sonic boom
detonator—
very loud

Knockout gas mechanism—
releases sleeping gas

Laser pointer—
useful for pointing
at things, cutting
through steel,
burning the eyes of
your enemy, etc.

Rocket mechanism—
stick on your back for
a cool jet-pack effect

Umbrella—
handy during
inclement weather or when
you're dropped from great
heights without a parachute

That sou...

Yeah, it's super unfortunate
none exists anywhere at all.
Definitely not in the mansion.
Definitely not in my secret stash
of adventure gear.

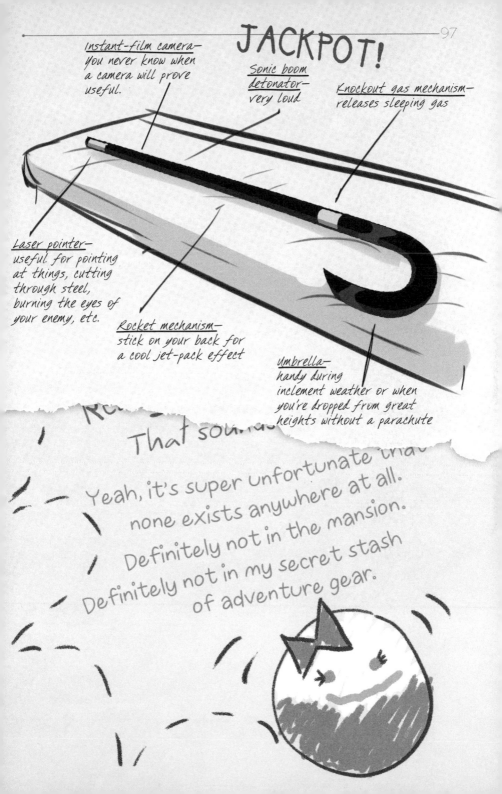

JUICE OF THE ANCIENTS FORMULA

...a Junior
Woodchuck badge all about
making gadgets! If
only you had
included a
diagram that
I could follow
to build one
myself....

Nice hat,
haha.

Why is this page torn out?

Is this a punch recipe?

Why are all adults so anti-punch???

THAT STUFF IS THE BEST!

It turns you into a mega bouncing ball.

Really?

That sounds awesome.

Yeah, it's super unfortunate that none exists anywhere at all. Definitely not in the mansion. Definitely not in my secret stash of adventure gear.

We were supposed to bid on a page torn from the Great Book of Castle Dunwyn and outbid Black Heron, a wily lass eager to obtain the page for F.O.W.L.

Hey! She doesn't have a robotic arm in this picture!

But why spend money when we could let Black Heron win the auction and steal it from her later? SAVED YOU SIXTY GRAND, YOU'RE WELCOME, S.H.U.S.H.!!!

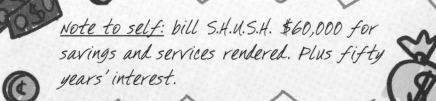

Note to self: bill S.H.U.S.H. $60,000 for savings and services rendered. Plus fifty years' interest.

Bonbon & Buttermilk Auction Catalog—1968

For over three hundred years, Bonbon & Buttermilk has been known the world over for brokering the sales of fine and decorative art, rare jewelry, antiques, mystical artifacts, cursed treasures, items of extraterrestrial origin, and fine decorative art.

Today's auction includes a plethora of spoils from all over the world curated to delight and inspire the discerning billionaire and to add a delightful pop to the assemblage of any serious collector.

Item 1: PAGE, GREAT BOOK — (circa Dark Ages, ca. 900 CE) This is the last page extracted from what is commonly referred to by scholars as the Great Book. The book was thought to have been lost forever until this ancient page was unearthed at the ruins of Castle Dunwyn. A priceless artifact for medieval enthusiasts or a rather curious page of decorative wrapping paper. Bidding will begin at £25,000.

Item 2: LAMP OF ETERNITY—(circa ... acquired from an area kn... discovered recently... lived there. ... sh... who ... firmed, its ... eight or creamer

...(circa 1949) Procured from ...its round objects, these square ...o have been laid by mystical chicken ...able and laced with salmonella (and are ...ption). Bidding will start at £5,000.

We tracked Black Heron to her secret hideout on an island in the Lairanas Trench, obtained the page, and fled the island before she could catch us. It was clear Beakley knew her stuff, and this was proven many times over as she worked undercover on a number of missions. Several years later, her identity would be compromised and Beakley would have to go into hiding. As it was clear she was good at cleaning up my messes, both literally and figuratively, I suggested she work for me as my housekeeper/bodyguard— and that has been her position ever since. She runs my home and keeps me sharp.

One morning, when Beakley was nowhere to be found, I scouted about and found an ungodly mess and a lone black feather. I knew right then that Black Heron was back.

Wait, where were we again?

I told you, watching the OTTOMAN EMPIRE marathon!

There was an awesome spy fight and we missed it???

OTHER IMPORTANT SPY GEAR

(Talk to Gyro; consider expanding, building into daily use.)

High-tech brooch—doubles as a homing device.

Granny wears a brooch!

I don't even know what a brooch is. It's that thing Granny wears!

Action cane 2.0—includes hot-water spigot and an adding machine for tallying savings acquired while on the job spying.

Does he mean a <u>calculator</u>?

Spats—deflect metal.

SPATS? No way. I think he should include a bow tie that SLICES through metal!

Yeah! And a watch that shoots out soda when you're thirsty! We should make our own list!

SPY STUFF THAT YOU WOULD ACTUALLY WANT/USE:

T-shirt—allows you to blend in perfectly with your surroundings, like a chameleon.

Pink hair bow—has a tiny deadly asp hidden inside.

Hat insert—doubles as a protractor, for perfect angle measuring.

Glove—doubles as a remote control, for hacking computer systems and changing the channel when you can't find the one for the TV.

As my submarine traveled back to the Lairanas Trench, I thought I was alone . . . until a nasty stowaway revealed herself!   Aw, so sweet! ♥

While I was concerned to have her along, I knew Webby was up for the challenge. After all, she had been trained by the best—me—and her grandmother was some help, too.

I was happy to see my lessons in action-cane wielding and grappling-hook utilization had paid off, and the wee lass made it to Black Heron's hideout in one piece. Once inside, we found Beakley . . . and Black Heron! Webby took copious notes as I swooped in and defeated Black Heron, saving the girl and her grandmother. We headed back to Duckburg with a quick stop at S.H.U.S.H. headquarters to deliver one Heron, plucked and stuffed.

WAIT A MINUTE! YOU FORGOT ALL THE GOOD STUFF! Remember when Black Heron was all, "Gimme the formula," and Granny was all, "Never!" and then Black Heron threatened to kill me so Granny gave it to her and then I KARATE CHOPPED and got the juice and I drank it and I bounced here and there and everywhere and then BLACK HERON drank it and we fought in the skies?!!!!!! AND YOU CALLED ME YOUR NEW PARTNER?!?!?!?! And I now call you Uncle Scrooge.

Also, you were just standing there pretty much the whole time, IIRC.

S.H.U.S.H.

Mission #482:
Agent McDuck and
Agent 22

That's my granny!

TOP SECRET

CLASSIFIED

Whoa, cool!!!

Guys, should we be looking at this? It seems like pretty important stuff, maybe we should leave it be.

JUST KIDDING, LET'S CHECK IT OUT!!!!!

S.H.U.S.H.

OBJECTIVE ONE: ████████████████

████████████████████████████████████

████████████████████████████████████

Can't talk about that.

Hey! Where's all the good stuff?!

OBJECTIVE TWO: ████████████████████

████████████████████████████████████

I think this case might still be open; should probably not include this, either.

OBJECTIVE THREE: ████████████████

████████████████████████████████████

████████████████████████████████████

I'd hate for this info to get into the wrong hands. Best to leave it out.

So he's not sharing ANYTHING top secret? What a waste!

I should have figured as much.

We never get to read anything fun.

My recent adventure with Webby has cemented my good impression of the girl. She's quick on her feet and quick with a punch. I'd say she's a mighty impressive specimen.

Whoa. Sorry, guys. I didn't mean to make you look bad My nephews I'm less impressed with. by looking so awesome.

Hmmm, that's not really a very good apology.

THE TRIPLETS' WEAKNESSES

Sorry about the bad apology, guys!

Dewey. Has a good golf swing. Could be a natural. Otherwise, too brash to be sensible. Weakness seems to be his poor poker face—I know he has a secret. I'll get to the bottom of it! Brash?! HE'S calling ME brash?!?!?! Has he EVER been in a dangerous situation with himself? He should take a good look in the mirror.

Louie. Smarty-pants. Keeping my good eye on him— may try to rob me blind. Weakness: lazy as all get-out. Likes to lie around. Also, likes to scheme.

Once again, nailed it.

Huey. Excellent at planning, to his own detriment. Weakness: doesn't trust himself or his abilities. Ditch that paperweight of a book! And what's that cap hiding? Even _I_ remove my top hat from time to time, despite all the many secrets it contains.

I have so many issues with this I don't know where to begin. And what's with his obsession with my hat?

CHAPTER NINE:
That Time I Stole Back My Treasure from Sky Pirates

My team and I were heading back from a fairly routine treasure-hunting expedition in Pato Pisco when a band of thieving scallywags intent on stealing my hard-won booty rudely accosted our flying vessel. These rapscallions insisted on being called Sky Pirates. As silly as that sounds, it's nothing compared to how silly they actually were.

Were they skilled thieves? Yes. They emptied out our plane in less than five minutes. Were they good pilots? Yes. Compared to Launchpad, they were _great_ pilots! Were they accomplished singers? "Singers?" you ask. "What does singing have to do with it?"

Well, it _should_ have nothing to do with it. This group of thieves insisted on making a fairly straightforward raid into a bloomin' Broadway musical! They were singing. They were dancing. They were twirling about so madly that I was frozen with befuddlement.

NO. Make that "frozen with _embarrassment._" I was embarrassed for the lot of 'em. But none more so than the supposed leader, the "dreaded DON Karnage." This supercilious piece of fluff must've tried his luck on the stage and been found wanting.

They say a picture's worth a thousand words, so here. I could say _more_ than a thousand words about this vociferous roaster. ~~To start with~~

On second thought, maybe I'll say zero words about this whole ludicrous affair.

Note to self: omit this chapter from the book!

I knew it! Typical Scrooge—the moment the spotlight's on someone else, he loses interest. Well, I'm de-omitting this chapter and calling it . . .

THE ADVENTURES OF CAPTAIN DEWEY!!

CAST OF CHARACTERS

CAPTAIN DEWEY!!—

Dashing. Daring. Darling. Dare I say more? I've got at least seven more adjectives beginning with "D," but I think you get the picture. The hero of our tale.

My old friend, the amazing and awesome alliteration!

DON KARNAGE

The "heavy" who's light on his feet. Does a mean box step and a mean bell kick. Also, he's just plain mean.

PEGLEG MEG

First mate to Captain Dewey. Executes his orders while in battle and on the dance floor. Special move: the infinite pirouette. Seriously, she can spin on her leg for hours.

STINKY BOOT

The first thing you notice about Stinky Boot is that he is well named. There is a distinct odor coming up from his feet. This is because he is constantly practicing his dance routine and never removes his footwear.

UGLY MUG

Actually prefers to be called Jitterbug. Another dance fanatic who immediately breaks into a Lindy Hop upon request. But don't ask him to hold a sword—he has permanent jazz hands.

ONE-EYED LINDA AND TWO-TOOTHED JACK

They pirate together. They dance together. They do everything together. Or they did, till Captain Dewey came along. Dare I say that

Linda has a crush on me? I Dewey dare it. Of course, just about every member of the crew has fallen for the debonair, dynamic captain. (Told you I had more "D" words....)

Wickedly wonderful!

Our Tale Begins....

Sky Pirates came swooping out of the sky, plundering Scrooge McDuck's plane and taking his treasure.
But while the rest of my cohorts were licking their
   wounds, I, Dewey Duck, staged a one-duck raid on
the pirates' plane.

   After defeating Captain Don Karnage in an epic
dance battle, I won the loyalty of the crew. They
   kicked Don to the curb and elected me their new
leader—The Dread Sky Pirate Dewey, Sky Scourge
of the Seven Skies!

But before I could begin what was sure to be
   a legendary career as a beloved pirate, I needed
   to right the wrong done to my family and return
Scrooge's treasure. So I told Pegleg Meg

Wow! And I thought Uncle Scrooge had trouble
 with facts. He may stretch the truth, but you've
ripped it in two, stomped on the remains, and lit
it on fire. I seem to remember it being <u>you</u> who
"wronged" the family, by taking us hostage and

I only did what I did because you guys wouldn't let
   me tell my story about Mount Peligroso! That's a
real story where I did really cool things! You never
give me a chance to tell it!

   Well, you just blew another chance right now.

DEAR MR. MCDEE,

WHILE HUEY AND DEWEY ARE ~~FIGHTING~~ WORKING THINGS OUT, i DECIDED TO PUT THIS PIRATE SONG iN HERE. i THINK iT'S A REAL TOE TAPPER AND WOULD MAKE A NiCE ADDITION TO YOUR AUTOBIOGRAPHY. i KNOW THAT WHEN i SiT DOWN TO READ, MY MiND TENDS TO WANDER AND i OFTEN START HEARING MUSIC iN MY HEAD. THIS WOULD BE A GREAT SONG FOR YOUR READERS' MiNDS TO WANDER TO!

SiNCERELY,

LAUNCHPAD

SKY PIRATES SONG

SKY PIRATES:

YO HO YO
YO HO YO
YO HO YO HO YO HO
AVAST YE LADS WHO BE FAINTHEARTED
WE RULE THESE SKIES UNCHARTED!
CRUEL AND VICIOUS HEARTIES WE
WHO SAIL UPON THE SKIES AND NOT THE SEA

DON KARNAGE:

TIS I WHO LEAD THIS FEARSOME CREW
WITH DAGGER, SWAGGER, DERRING-DO!
HANDSOME, AND FEARSOME, AND SUAVE

SKY PIRATES:

HE'S THE FAMOUS PIRATE CAPTAIN

SKY PIRATES & DON KARNAGE:

DON KARNAGE! HA HA

SKY PIRATES & DON KARNAGE:

HOIST THE FLAG AND WEIGH THE ANCHOR
CIRCLE THE SHIP AND PULL TO FLANK 'ER

SKY PIRATES:

HI-HO, HE LIVES TO PLUNDER!

DON KARNAGE:

IT''S TRUE, I LIVE TO PLUNDER

SKY PIRATES:

HIGH UP IN THE SKY
AMIDST A SEA OF STORM AND THUNDER

DON KARNAGE:

NOW BACK TO ME, THE MAIN EVENT!
A PERNICIOUS, VICIOUS, RAKISH GENT
A FRUSTRATINGLY CHARMING BLAGGART

SKY PIRATES:

HE'LL STEAL YOUR TREASURE AND YOUR HEART!

DON KARNAGE:

AND NOW WE DANCE. HA HA

SKY PIRATES:

HE'S DON KARNAGE

DON KARNAGE:

THAT'S ME!

SKY PIRATES:

IT'S DON KARNAGE

DON KARNAGE:

STILL ME! AH HA HA HA

SKY PIRATES & A PARROT:

PILFER THE LOOT TO FILL OUR COFFERS
BEEN A PLEASURE TO TAKE IT OFF YA
WE PUT ON A SHOW, THEN STEAL YOUR DOUGH
THEN INTO THE CLOUDS, AWAY WE GO

DON KARNAGE:

TO THE CLOUDS, AWAY I GO

SKY PIRATES & DON KARNAGE:

YO-HO!

There is one thing worthy of praise in the (omitted) tale of the Sky Pirates—their bonny flying machines!

I've always had a soft spot in my heart for a well-designed aeroplane. Probably because I was around when the whole bleeding idea of mechanical flying <u>got off the ground!</u>

Boy, you sure do love these bad puns.

There were a fair number of dead-end designs and doomed flights before the Wright brothers made their successful voyage (with financial backing from yours truly). A few noteworthy examples:

<u>The Prettyhawk</u>—Some good design decisions, but relying on captured birds as a power source is a bit of a cheat.

The Quintuple-Decker—

If two wings are good, then ten wings must be five times better, right? Wrong. Very wrong. Disastrously wrong.

The Pogocopter—

This machine reached an altitude of seven hundred feet before dropping down to zero feet then bouncing back up to six hundred and fifty feet and dropping back down to, well, you get the idea.

The Air Beater—

This contraption went nowhere. But it did make a mean scrambled egg.

Speaking of eggs, I need Beakley to fill the pantry. We are getting dangerously low on supplies!

Grocery List

Haggis

Biscuits

Tea

Day-old bread—or _two_-day-old bread (if they have it!)

Bruised apples (Remind her to haggle for a discount.)

~~Anything for the kids?~~   ←YES!

Things for "The Kids"

(How many times do I need to make this list?)

<u>Cereal</u>—Including (but not limited to) Nutso Puffs, Shredded Skateboards, and All-Sweet Syrup Bombs.

Might want to order some extras, so we can use the boxes to build a cereal box bin.

<u>Milk for cereal</u>—No, we cannot just "pour water on it."

Did somebody say <u>cheap?</u>

<u>Juices</u>—Vitamin D-licious Orange-Flavored Juice Infusion. And Crock-ade X-treme.

AND Cherry Pep, Berry Pep, Blueberry Pep, Snozberry Pep, Neapolitan Pep, French Riviera Pep, Arctic Blast Pep, and Antarctic Blast Pep.

(FYI: Five-liter bottles are the best bargain—just looking out for your budget, Uncle Scrooge.)

Yeah, me too. . . . Plus, the more money you save, the more money you have to give me!

<u>Chips</u>—Must have pretzels, corn chips, and potato puffs. Must be flavored with lemon-lime, ranch, jalapeño, and/or honey barbecue Buffalo cheddar.

<u>Dessert</u>—Ice cream: any/all flavors. Chocolate sauce. Marshmallows. Sprinkles AND jimmies (they are two different things)! I'm fine with just taking my ice cream with gold coin toppings.

PLEASE NOTE: <u>ALL</u> of the above are essential parts of a well-balanced diet for growing kids!

It's probably time to expand McDuck Enterprises to match the newly expanded range of my adventures. . . .

McDuck Enterprises Departments to Create/Reinstate:

-Historical Research—Though I've made quite a bit of history myself!

-Risk Management—I'd rather call it "Risk Encouragement," but the bean counters would scream.

-Experimental Tech—Hopefully getting his own department will keep Gyro out of my hair.

-Magical Totems and Ephemera—Time to stop storing this junk in my garage.

-Deep Sea Exploration—I'd bet a dollar that Atlantis isn't the only underwater city out there! And I don't take betting money lightly.

Junk to Get out of the Garage

1) Triceratops skeleton

2) Caveduck skeleton

3) Chupacabra skeleton **I knew he was real!**

4) Stone Scrooge statue

5) Gong of Pixiu

6) Medusa Gauntlet **I call dibs when he dies!**

7) Cursed Chest of Captain Peghook, the Scourge
   of the River Styx

8) The Deus Excalibur

9) Saddle of the Headless Man-horse

10) Jewel of Atlantis

11) Druid Cup **This is technically mine.**

12) Khopesh of Toth-Ra **And this is technically Launchpad's!**

Will need to give this list to Beakley so she can move
this stuff to the warehouse. . . .

Sure . . . "Moving" the dangerous mystical stuff into a "warehouse." Of course. . . .

Are you trying to write something that sounds sassy and sly and "in the know"?

"In the know"? No! I mean, what is there to know? I don't know anything. I don't—

All right, we're going to stop you right there. We know there's another bin where Scrooge keeps all the dangerous magical doodads and what not.

And we know that you and Lena found it and broke in.

What? How did you find out? Who told you?

You did. Immediately. Like, minutes after you got back.　Oh, yeah. . . . Whoops.

You'd think that, with all the magical tools I have at my disposal, my every need would be met. That's where you would be ridiculously wrong. Dealing with magic is a tricky proposition. There's always some "fine print" when it comes to spells and curses. There's only one way to do each one right and so many ways they can go wrong.

In short, I don't trust magic. It's best to rely on good old-fashioned hard work and good old-fashioned science.

Science sounds so boring when compared to magic, you say? Well, then, you haven't met my resident genius, Gyro Gearloose!

Gyro is the foremost mind working in advanced technology and biomechanics. And he works for me! With my visionary leadership and Gyro's ingenuity, McDuck Enterprises has become a hub for technological innovation. Our successes are legendary and have received their fair amount of praise in the popular press. But there are a few orphaned projects I might want to "plug" in this book to help them get back off the ground. . . .

<u>Automatic Yo-Yos</u>: No skill needed. Just flip a switch and watch them go! These little guys worked like a charm. But when you "walked the dog," the yo-yo went for a long walk and never came back.

<u>Self-Folding Shirts</u>: For the traveling business individual who doesn't have time to pack. Unfortunately, before you had time to catch your flight, the shirts would start flapping their arms and fly away on their own.

<u>Lie-to-Me Mirrors</u>: These were supposed to make everyone look more attractive, but due to a manufacturing flaw, they had more of a random and terrifying warped funhouse mirror effect.

Putting this on my birthday list.

<u>Early Microwave Oven</u>:
We had this technology years ahead of our competitors. Our prototype heated food quite well. But the radiation also changed the food into small and powerful ogre-like creatures. Your casserole would beat you up before you could bite it.

<u>Bulb-Tech</u>: Gyro has a lot of faith in this unproven technology, but so far, all his first prototype, Li'l Bulb, has done is try to kill us all on two (or is it three?) separate occasions. I say we gift wrap the little guy and send him to Glomgold.

~~Project Blatherskite~~ ~~Now here's a project that I~~
~~have more faith in than Gyro. Duckburg could use~~

Hah! You can't fool me, Uncle Scrooge! You're talking about Gizmoduck—Duckburg's new superhero and close personal friend of yours truly!

Are you talking about that failed robot butler app/costume that Mark Beaks from Waddle tried launching?

There is so much wrong in that sentence that I don't know where to begin.

Not a butler—a superhero.

Not a robot—a cybernetic suit of armor.

You sooo wanna be his sidekick. . . .

That's ridiculous. I mean, if he'd have me . . . Why, what have you heard?

I hate you right now.

Scrooge's Ramblings

How to brew a proper cup of tea: (This is gonna be good, I can feel it!)

-Boil water. A good, rolling boil. For kindling, I like to use money from countries suffering from severe inflation (rarely worth the paper it's printed on, but use what works for you.   Use adult supervision!

-Pick a tea. Tea is one of the few things I splurge on, allowing myself to drop anywhere from a dime to a quarter a bag. But while that sounds wildly extravagant, I also like to . . .

-Reuse the tea bag and taste the savings! I can usually get a month's worth of tea from one bag.

-Don't bother with sugar, milk, or lemon. Straight tea supports steely nerves.

Louie's Life Lessons (patent pending): Drink Cherry Pep instead of gross old leaves in a bag.

CHAPTER TEN:
My Immortal Parents
(And How I Finally Earned Their Respect)

HOORAY!
A TIME LINE!
Definitely needs to be fact-checked
against my McDuck Mystery Board.

Time Line of My Ancestors:

EIDER (946 CE)
Killed defending castle from Anglo-Saxons. His serfs deserted him because he was cheap.

QUACKLY (1057)
Trapped in a wall trying to hide treasure earned from defending King Macbeth.

MURDOCH (1066)
Developed the longbow patent; made his fortune selling longbows to the English and charging extra for the arrows; killed by longbow.

STUFT (1189)
Prosperous; died wealthy.

ROAST (1205)
Stupidly gave family treasure to England; ate himself to death.

SWAMPHOLE (1220)
Made back money, hoarded his treasure, built passageways in Castle McDuck, then closed them off and summoned a "demon dog" to stand watch.

BLACK DONALD (1440)
Invented golf. Subsequently got it banned.

SIMON (1500)
Secretary/accountant of Knights Templar; stole their treasure and hid it in the castle.

1675—Family lost castle after being chased away by a devil dog (conjured by the Whiskervilles).

SEAFOAM (1727)
Sailor/buccaneer who plundered treasure.

1800s—Scrooge helped family buy back castle and rid the castle of the Whiskervilles.

SILAS (1800s)
Silas conned Druids out of building a new Stonehenge on McDuck land. These must be the same Druids who supplied the mystical stones Scrooge used to rebuild and curse the castle!

DIRTY DINGUS (1800s)
Fergus's dad; coal miner. Couldn't pay taxes.

Hahaha

Haahaha

I don't get it.

FERGUS AND DOWNEY MCDUCK
Father and mother of Scrooge McDuck. As residents of Castle McDuck, are unfortunate immortals because the castle was rebuilt with mystical Druid stones that Scrooge got cheap.

If you REALLY want to know the history of Clan McDuck, you need to go to the source: me. I know EVERYTHING there is to know about Scrooge McDuck! Check out my McDuck Mystery Board!

This is terrifyingly elaborate.

But also thoroughly researched.

Every five years, the mists of the Moors of Dismal Downs part and reveal:

My ancestral home.
CASTLE MCDUCK.

A place as ancient as Scotland itself, full of riddles, mystery, dangers, and a rogue ghost or two.

Don't forget INSANELY TERRIFYING DEMON DOGS.

They weren't _that_ scary.

WHAT?!?

There was treasure involved.
Greed trumps fear.

It's also the location of the Lost Treasure of the Knights Templar.

I return every five years when the mists clear to claim the treasure hidden away within the castle walls. But the treasure is guarded by immortals, and those immortals guarding it are too terrifying for words.

Did I mention the immortals are my own mummy and daddy? Downey and Fergus McDuck. That's right: they'll live forever. And they're always on my case about it.

This painting just makes me chuckle.

This is the best.
What a **sucker** (pun intended).
Uncle Donald looks so ridiculous!

unfortunately for me, my father—as laird of the castle—determines who is worthy of the treasure, so I had to be on my best behavior. Hard to do with that moldy old codger insulting me at every turn!

So I did what I always do, because I'm tougher than the toughies and smarter than the smarties: I set out to find the treasure myself! When I went off, my dad, always eager for a handout, followed along, hoping to ride my coattails to success.

As we searched through the castle together, I saw a different side of my father. I soon realized it was he who instilled the value of hard work and self-reliance in me, something I hope to instill in those young lazy nephews of mine who are getting a bit soft. Especially Louie. Hey!

We searched through the castle and found what we'd assumed was the treasure, only to learn my grandpappy got the best of us both. I vowed to return in another five years to search for the treasure with my dad.

BUT WAIT! DON'T END THE CHAPTER! I STILL HAVE SO MANY QUESTIONS!
Save it for another five years, Webby.

Number One Dime

How can a dime be a symbol of success? When its worth is more than the number stamped on it. As a young entrepreneur in Scotland, I set out with a homemade shoeshine kit, determined to earn my keep to help at home. I worked on old Burt the ditchdigger's shoes for hours, and in exchange he gave me an American dime. ~~But then I learned the true origin of the dime~~ Why is this part crossed out? What's he hiding about that dime? Don't ask.

Working for that dime taught me my true worth. Nothing felt as good as the full-body exhaustion I experienced while slaving away for a coin I couldn't even spend in my own country. It encouraged me to follow my dreams to America, which led me down the path to being the richest duck in the world.

UGH, he never lets up about that dime.

Hey, has anyone ever seen the back of the dime?

Nope.

Nope.

Uh-uh.

Hmmmm...

Ways to Keep
Number One Dime Safe

Again with that dime!

Have many replicas made. I know the true
Number One Dime because it has ███████
████████████████████████████

Coat dime in toxic wax that burns the skin.
Put protective wax on my fingers.
Hypothetically, where would one acquire this toxic wax?

Build a safe devoted to the dime. Keep safe in
larger safe. Keep larger safe in money bin.

Rig an eardrum-piercing alarm. Don't forget
earplugs.

Create a (velvet death pillow) for the dime to
reside on. _↓ Another Daft Duck album title option._

Swallow dime. As I only move my bowels every
third Sunday, its whereabouts will be easy
to track.

Ewwwwww!!!!!

Never
eat money.

<u>Scrooge's (Scottish) Scramblings</u>

How to write a proper Scottish poem:

-Every good Scotsman worth his weight in coin will have a litany of verbiage at his disposal. And when he's at a loss, he'll rely on a series of guttural sounds to throw off opposing parties.

-Add a mild insult. It shows you didn't come to dally, you mean business.

-Try to rhyme. And when you can't rhyme, yell.

Things every Scotsman should know about <u>tartan</u>:

-It's not PLAID. Don't call it PLAID.

-Tartan is made of pre-dyed threads woven at right angles to each other. Don't doodle with some markers on a sheet and call it tartan.

-If you aren't Clan McDuck, you can't wear Clan McDuck tartan. Period.

Conclusion

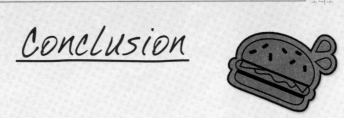

Well, it looks like I've just about run out of pages, but we are far from running out of adventures.

It's been an epic time with more pursuits of treasure to follow. Will my adventuring ever stop? The question's been asked time and time again, usually by Beakley as she scrubs the stains out of my spats.

SCRAPPY?!?!

I can't seem to shake these scrappy bairns who I call kin. It looks like I'll be in it for the long haul. And why not? They deserve to learn from the best how adventuring is truly done. But are they cut out for it? Are they made from the stuff of legends?

ALL RIGHT, ALL RIGHT, we get it. You don't like adventuring with us. No need to go on about it!

The Children's Strengths

Wait, what?

To be a good adventurer, you've got to be smarter than the smarties, like HUEY. Calculating and deducing, he's always a step ahead.

Aw, thanks, Uncle Scrooge.

To be a good adventurer, you've got to be tougher than the toughies, like DEWEY. What some might read as impetuous, I read as fearless.

Well, I try.

To be a good adventurer, you've got to be sharper than the sharpies, like LOUIE. His gift of gab can smooth any rough patch he comes across.

THANK YOU. I've been saying this all along!

To be a good adventurer, you've got to make your way square, like WEBBY. Honest and forthright, she's the one you want on your team because you know she'll have your back.

Guys, I'm starting to feel squishy inside!

I've vented about their (many) flaws several times. But these overwhelming strengths overshadow any shortcomings.

When these four get together, they're unstoppable. And it makes me proud.

Is anyone else confused?

Yeah—he's being nice!

A little too nice. I don't trust it.

It makes me even prouder to know I just got them to read an entire book! Kept their eyes OFF THE MIND-MELTING TELLY FOR A BIT and got them learning a thing or two!

There it is.

Wait. What's happening in my brain? I think it's . . . growing. Is this . . . LEARNING?

NOOOOOOOOOOOOOOOOOOOOOO!!!!!!!!

Will this count for my Junior Woodchuck Copyediting Badge?

Now, kids, get your nosy noses out of my notebook and get on the plane. It's time to find the Maltese MacGuffin!!!!

Family is the
greatest
adventure of all!